Meet the Teeth

Dr. Ted M. Pinney

Illustrated by Ronie Pios

Order this book online at www.trafford.com
or email orders@trafford.com

Most Trafford titles are also available at major online book retailers.

Printed in the United States of America.

ISBN: 9781490744483 (sc)
         9781490744476 (e)

Library of Congress Control Number: 2014914649

Trafford rev.: 08/15/2014

www.trafford.com

North America & international
toll-free: 1 888 232 4444 (USA & Canada)
fax: 812 355 4082

Meet Tatum, she is six years old.
This is Tyler, Tatum's ten-year-old brother.

Tatum and Tyler are just like any other children. They like to play outside. They love to have fun with their friends.

They even get along well with each other sometimes.

In this story, we are going to take a closer look at Tatum and Tyler. We are going to see what goes on in their mouths.

EWWW!

YUCK!

Really???

I know, I know, it sounds kind of gross. But I think you will enjoy learning about the teeth and what goes on, not just in Tatum's and Tyler's mouth but also in yours.

SO, LETS MEET THE TEETH

Tatum first:
Hello, my name is Rip. I am a baby tooth called a central incisor. My job is to tear into food.

Soon, me and my baby tooth friends will get loose and fall out to be replaced by permanent teeth.

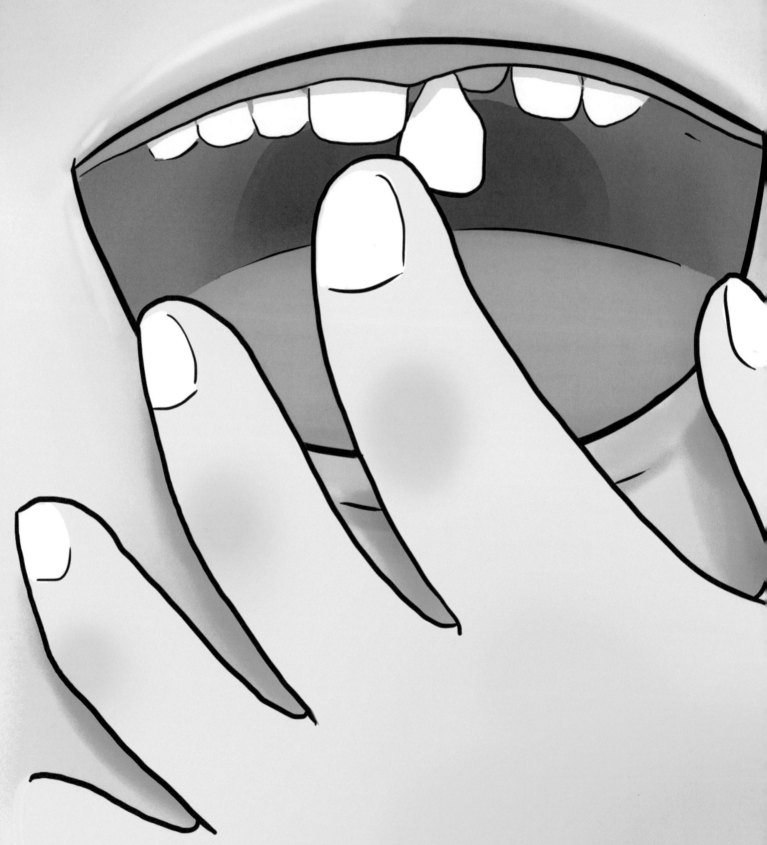

I would like to introduce you to some of my friends. Right next to me is Cinderellat. She is a lateral incisor and her job is just like mine.

Next to Cinderellat is Vamp the canine. He pierces food with his point or cusp.

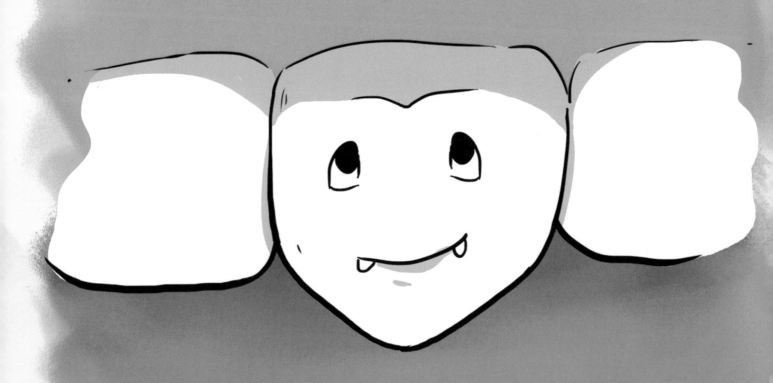

In the back are molars. This guy's name is Moley. He crushes and grinds food so they can be swallowed.

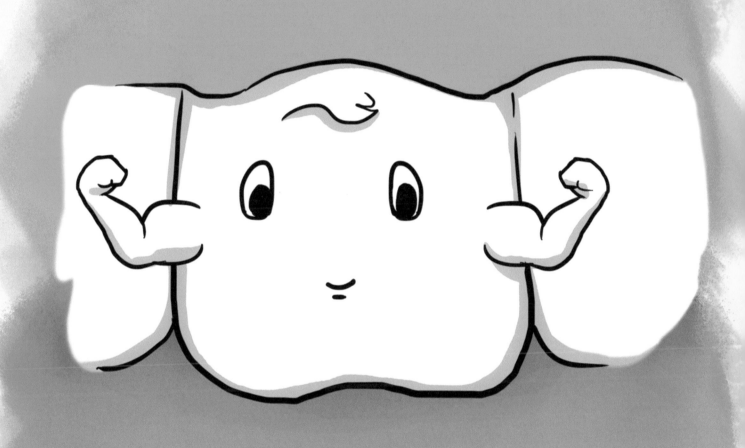

Hey, Moley, I see a dark spot in your groove. We need to get to the dentist so you can be filled.

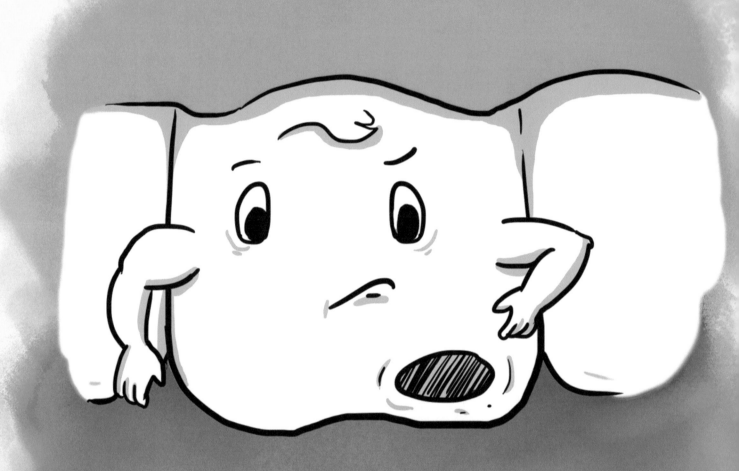

It's very important to visit the dentist twice a year to get us cleaned and checked for cavities like the one Moley has.

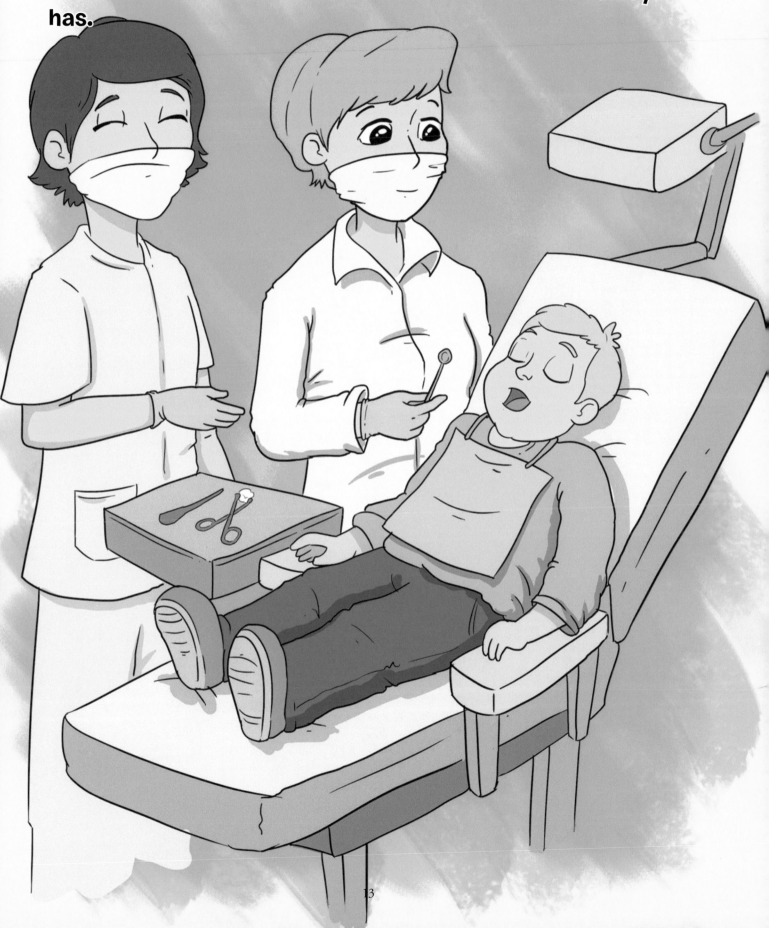

That big guy below me, we like to call him Mister Clean. He is the tongue which has many uses. For teeth, he helps keep us clean by removing stuff left on us after we chew food.

One of our favorite times of the day is bath time. You call this brushing your teeth.

We get brushed twice a day for two minutes each time.

That was Tatum's mouth. Let's check out Tyler's teeth.
I am Rip Sr. I am a permanent central incisor.

Tyler is nine, so he has some permanent and some baby teeth.

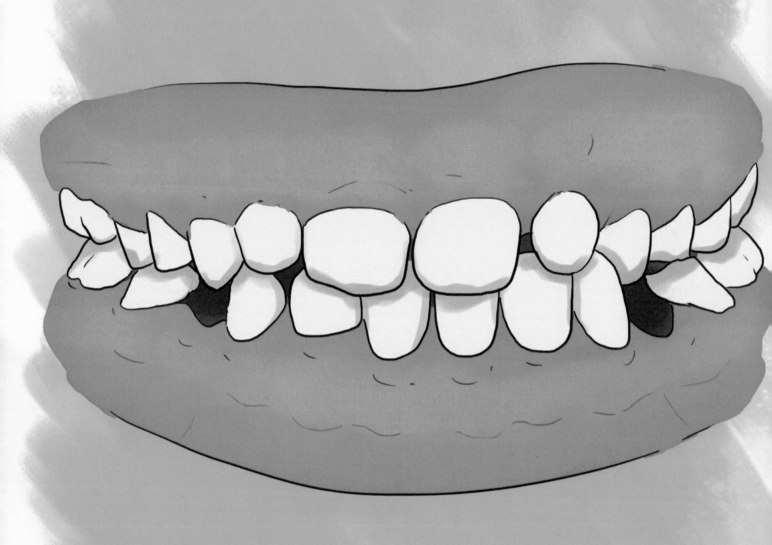

All the way to the back, you see Perm. She is a permanent six-year molar. She is one of the first permanent teeth to enter or erupt in each child's mouth right around the age of six.

With permanent teeth, flossing and brushing us becomes more important. Flossing cleans between teeth where brushing can't reach.

Let's review some important things about your teeth:

    - Visit a dentist twice a year to get your teeth cleaned and checked.

    - Brush your teeth twice a day for two minutes each time.

    - Floss every day especially when you get your permanent teeth.

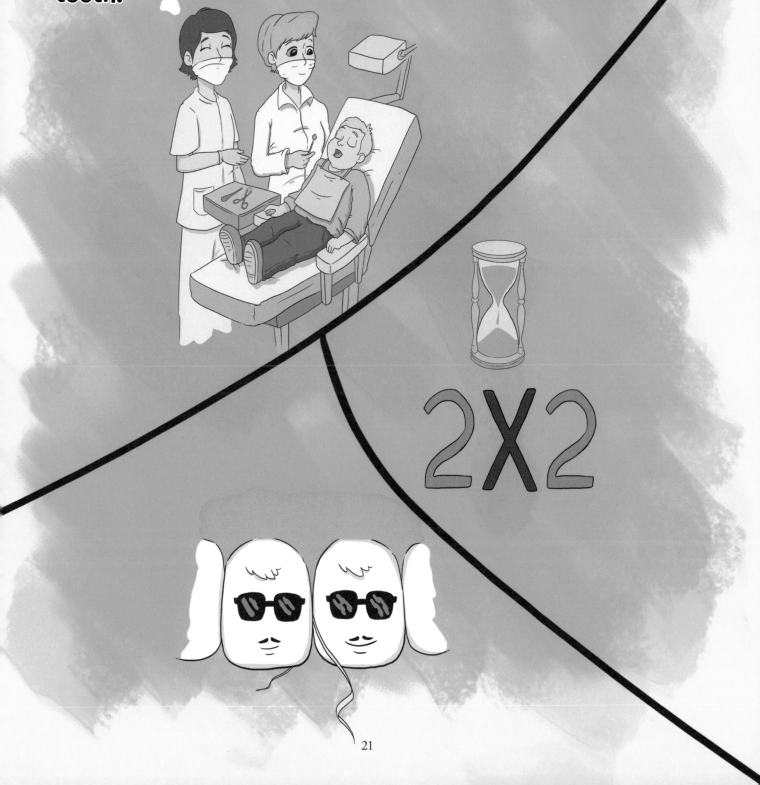

Thank you for joining us in this adventure *Meet the Teeth*.

The end

About the book

It is a book about dental anatomy and dental hygiene. The book introduces two children of two different ages and then zooms in to show their teeth and some of their characteristics. The teeth become characters themselves. It discusses functions and anatomy and brushing guidelines.

About the Author

Dr Ted Pinney is a practicing general dentist in Jacksonville, AR. He has been in practice for 10 years and is a 3rd generation dentist. He has always wanted to write a book that would educate children and be fun at the same time. His goal with *"Meet The Teeth"* is to do just that. He is inspired by his wife Christie and their two children Tyler and Tatum who appear in the book.

Printed in the United States
by Baker & Taylor Publisher Services